£5.25

ANNUAL

Britt Allcroft's THOMAS THE TANK ENGINE & FRIENDS based on The
Railway Series by The Rev W Awdry

Photographic stills and illustrations
© Britt Allcroft (Thomas) Limited 1992, 1995

Storyline © William Heinemann Limited 1995

THOMAS THE TANK ENGINE & FRIENDS is a trademark of Britt Allcroft
(Thomas) Limited

All publishing and underlying copyright worldwide William Heinemann Limted.
All television and merchandising rights licensed by William Heinemann Limited
to Britt Allcroft (Thomas) Limited exclusively worldwide.

Published by
GRANDREAMS LIMITED
Jadwin House 205-211 Kentish Town Road
London NW5 2JU

Printed in Italy

CONTENTS

Hello! My name is Mavis. I work for the Quarry Company. I have shiny black paint and six small wheels, protected by side plates. Toby says I've still got a lot to learn about trucks but I think he's a fusspot. Of course I know what I'm doing, I'm a smart diesel engine - and I'm much younger than he is! But I do miss Toby when he's not around, as you will find out when you read our story inside.

The Fat Controller said I am the youngest engine to introduce the Thomas Annual. Because the other engines were busy he said it would be really useful indeed if I could help. I was very nervous to begin with, but Toby showed me what to do. So, more about what's inside...

As well as lots of exciting activities to keep you busy, there are stories to enjoy about your favourite engines - there's the time the Island of Sodor is thrown into darkness after a power cut. James finds out about pancakes. A school football match causes trouble for Thomas and Toby and I have difficulty at the quarry, but everything is forgotten on Christmas Eve when a pantomime is performed in the station yard!

Have fun now!

James Gets Cracking

It was a bright, spring morning when James puffed importantly into the yard. The Fat Controller had an unusual job for him today.

"Well done James," he said, "I see you have plenty of steam already."

"Yes Sir," replied James eagerly.

"That means you can set off right away," said the Fat Controller.

"Where to Sir?" asked James.

"To the battery farm," said the Fat Controller.

James' driver climbed out of the cab to talk with the Fat Controller. James couldn't hear what they were saying, but he tried hard to listen because he was puzzled. James hadn't heard of a farm for batteries before! He'd seen the signal man put batteries in his transistor radio, to listen to the weather forecast, but he didn't think they came from a farm.

James was soon pulling hard up the hill, away from the station yard. "A battery farm, a battery farm," he puffed to the trucks.

"It's not far now James," called his driver. "Farmer Finney is meeting us at Tidmouth!"

As they pulled into the station, they saw the farmer waiting on the platform with

lots of wooden crates. The crates were loaded carefully into one of James' trucks. Farmer Finney waved them off. "Take care," he called.

"Why do we have to take care of batteries?" James spluttered to himself.

"Come on James," shouted his driver. "We have to deliver this to the school by 10 o'clock!" So James went full steam along the track. But there was something up ahead. A line of hens were flapping about on the track!

"Stop! Stop! Stop!" called James, as his driver leaned hard on the brake lever. With a bang and a clunk, James stopped just in time, but his poor truck was thrown off the rails and broken eggs lay everywhere. "What a mess!" sighed James' driver.

"Eggs!" said James in surprise. "I thought they were batteries!"

James' driver laughed. "Farmer Finney keeps hens and chickens who lay lots of eggs. That sort of farm is called a battery farm," he explained. James did feel silly.

They were interrupted by the sound of Terence the Tractor. Farmer Finney had come to see what had happened. He was surprised to see that some of his chickens had escaped and sorry that they had caused an accident. "What can I do to help?" he said.

"You could deliver some more eggs to the school, while we get help," suggested James' driver. "The children need them to make pancakes."

The farmer agreed. "I'll hook a trailer up to Terence and drive slowly so that no more eggs get broken!"

It was a day of surprises for James. While the railway staff helped put the truck back on the rails, the driver told James all about Shrove Tuesday.

"People make a batter using eggs and cook it in a big frying pan to make delicious pancakes. The school children are making pancakes today in their cookery lesson," he said.

When the farmer returned he had something in his hand. It was a frying pan. "A pancake!" exclaimed James.

"With lemon and sugar!" said the driver.

The children had made them a special pancake. So before they got back to work, the driver, the farmer and the workmen shared the big pancake and James looked on happily.

Can you spot ten differences between these two pictures of Bulgy and his passengers?

Answers on pages 44 and 45.

Here is a summertime picture to colour. Can you spot the Fat Controller amongst this seaside crowd?

TEAS

ICE CREAM

1

Answers on pages 44 and 45.

Percy and Duck

Rings A Bell!

Henry was having trouble getting his trucks to behave. They bumped and squealed as he dragged them to the quarry for Mavis and Toby. The troublesome trucks didn't want to be filled up with scratchy stones and they wouldn't let Henry forget it! But Henry knew his difficult journey was nearly over when he heard the ring of his friend's bell.

"Poop, poop! Hello Toby!"

he called.

At the quarry, things were very disorganised. Mavis was squabbling with some trucks and Toby was nowhere to be seen.

"You seem behind with your work Mavis," said Henry's driver. "Never mind, I'm sure Toby will be here soon."

"I expect so," sulked Mavis, who didn't like Toby helping her all the time. She wanted to do things on her

own.

"Toby's an old fusspot," she said, bumping a line of trucks crossly.

She didn't want Henry's help either, so he returned to the station yard - glad to leave the mess behind!

The next morning it was Edward's turn to take empty trucks to the quarry. He was looking forward to seeing his old friend Toby. As Edward steamed carefully along the outlying quarry line he heard the ring of Toby's bell.

"Hello Toby!" he called. But Edward didn't get a reply.

When Edward arrived at the quarry, he had never seen such a mess. Mavis bumped a truck so hard that it broke and the rest of the trucks were refusing to work.

"Toby will help you," said Edward kindly.

"I don't want his help," snapped Mavis. "I can do it

on my own."

"Where is Toby?" asked Edward.

"Oh! Somewhere I expect!" replied Mavis.

"Wherever he is, it must be important for him to leave you in this mess," said Edward's driver.

"I'm not in a mess!" said Mavis, as the poor truck collapsed in front of her sending white chalky dust everywhere.

That afternoon, Thomas waited for Mavis to bring the loaded trucks down to the station yard, but they didn't arrive. Thomas' driver spoke to the Fat Controller. "There must be something wrong," he said.

The Fat Controller was very concerned and decided to go to the quarry himself. Thomas took him right away. On the way they heard Toby's bell ring.

"Stop here please!" said the Fat Controller. "I'd like to check that Toby isn't in trouble."

The Fat Controller was surprised by what he found on the other side of the hedge. It

was a big cow wearing a cow-bell around her neck! They carried on to the quarry and there they found Mavis surrounded by derailed trucks and covered in dust. She didn't expect a visit from the Fat Controller.

"What on earth....!" he cried. "Where's Toby?"

Poor Mavis was so fed up, she started to cry.

"I haven't seen him all day," she sniffed.

"Well you should have told someone," said the Fat Controller, more kindly. He was

not cross with Mavis now because he could see she was sorry.

Thomas took the Fat Controller to Toby's shed and inside stood poor Toby with a broken wheel. He thought all his friends had forgotten about him.

"We thought we heard your bell!" said Thomas. "But it was a cow!"

The Fat Controller agreed that when Toby's wheel was mended he would give him a brand new bell so that they would always recognise him.

Who will find the lost truck in the quarry?

Answers on pages 44 and 45.

20

Can you find ten top hats like this one in the picture?

Answers on pages 44 and 45.

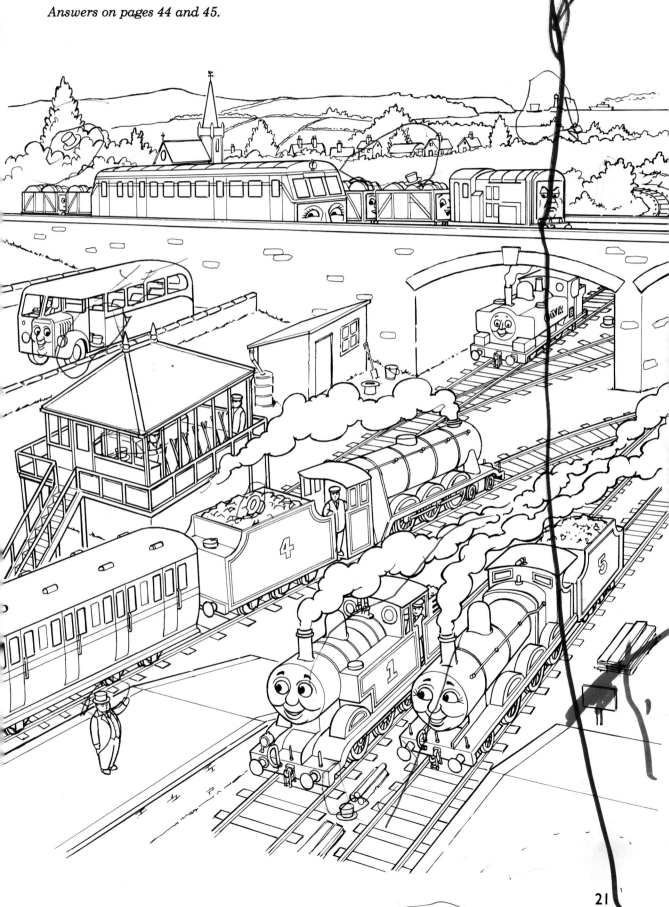

21

The Railway Game

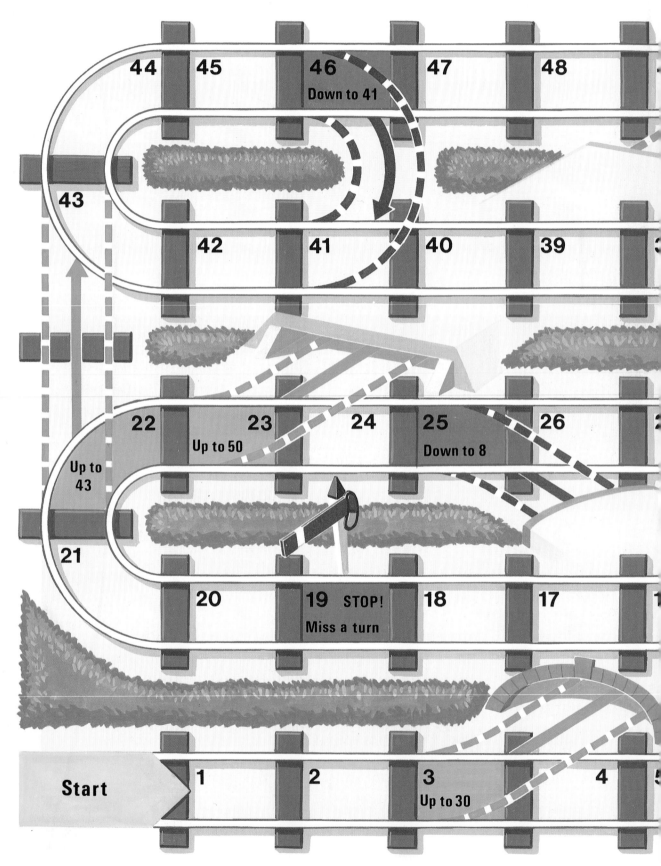

44 45 46 **Down to 41** 47 48

43

42 41 40 39

22 23 **Up to 50** 24 25 **Down to 8** 26

Up to 43

21

20 19 **STOP! Miss a turn** 18 17

Start 1 2 3 **Up to 30** 4

A game for two or more players. You will need counters and a dice. Throw the dice and move the number of places shown. If you land on a coloured section of the rail track, follow the instruction. See who can reach the end of the line first.

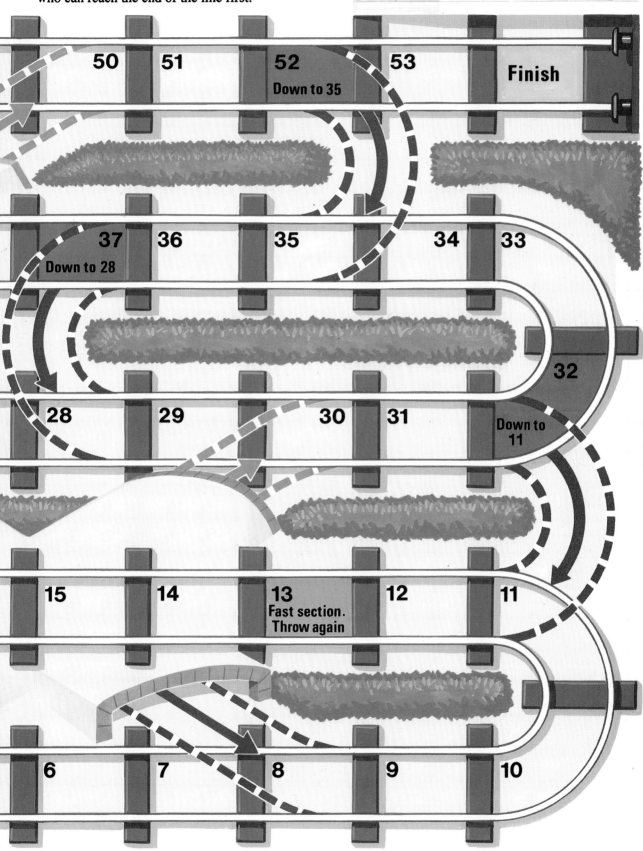

50 **51** **52**
Down to 35
53 **Finish**

37 **36** **35** **34** **33**
Down to 28

32

28 **29** **30** **31**
Down to 11

15 **14** **13** **12** **11**
Fast section.
Throw again

6 **7** **8** **9** **10**

Toby and Daisy

All Pull Together

A cold, wintry wind blew down Oliver's funnel as he rushed to the harbour with Toad.

"Brrr," said his driver. "It looks as if a storm is blowing over from the mainland."

Oliver didn't like storms. The wind reminded him of a lonely night he spent once in a shed waiting to be scrapped. But that was a long time ago and he was saved by his friends, so he put the thought right out of his mind and hurried to the harbour with his load.

"Hello Oliver," peeped Percy as he fought against the wind.

"Do you need some help?" called Oliver.

"Yes," said Percy.

It was so gusty that Percy's post train had been delayed. There were letters everywhere - they had blown right out of the trucks! Luckily, Oliver had some rope so, together, the drivers secured the post sacks to Percy's trucks.

Percy was all ready to go when a big rumble, louder than Gordon rushing through a tunnel, thundered around them. Percy closed his eyes tight.

"What is it?" shuddered Oliver.

"It's thunder," his driver replied. "No need to worry!"

But even the driver jumped when jagged lightning flashed across the sky. When Percy and Oliver opened their eyes again they were in complete darkness. The lights in the harbour yard had all gone out.

"Cinders and ashes," squealed Percy. "Where am I?"

"You're in the same place as before, but you can't see it - that's all!" said Oliver kindly.

The harbour master telephoned the Fat Controller to find out what to do. When he returned to the yard he had important instructions for Oliver and Percy. "There has

27

been a power cut on the island," he said. "We need your help."

"Yes," said Percy and Oliver bravely.

The harbour master continued, "You must deliver candles to every station so that passengers can find their way around the railway so we can stay open."

Percy and Oliver soon set off with their unusual load. Oliver took the coast line and Percy headed inland.

Percy made good time, but he had to stop at a level crossing. There he met Bertie the Bus, taking an engineer to the electricity cable that had been damaged in the storm.

When Percy arrived at Wellsworth, it was very busy. Railway lamps hung outside the station to light the way and some of Percy's candles were unloaded to light the waiting room. Percy thought the flickering flames looked very cosy indeed. He was sorry

to leave, but there was more to do.

Meanwhile, Oliver passed the airfield and was surprised to see Harold the Helicopter flying in the storm.

"I'm on an important mission!" said Harold boldy.

Oliver watched Harold lift a broken tree branch off the power cable and into the air. Then Bertie arrived with the engineer and he climbed up to the cable with his tool kit.

The cable was soon mended and all around lights came back on. Everything was bright again. Oliver heard the happy sound of people cheering in the distance.

Later that night, outside the shed, the Fat Controller thanked Oliver, Percy, Bertie and Harold for being so brave. "You have all been really useful and I am very proud of you. By all pulling together we have saved the island from a very dark night," he said proudly.

Join the dots to see what is alarming Thomas and his crew.

Can you match the correct halves of the Vicar?

Answers on pages 44 and 45.

1   A

2   E

3   B

4   C

5   F

6   D

PETER SAM

A hard worker, Peter Sam is a happy and kindly engine. His vulnerability means he is often teased by the others, but deep down he is a popular engine and loved by all.

RUSTY

Fearless and determined, Rusty is a self assured engine who enjoys an adventure. A friend to all, Rusty has a huge heart.

DUKE

The oldest of the Narrow Gauge engines, Duke uses his experience to maintain authority with the younger engines. He enjoys teaching, and is a gentle and kind engine to look up to.

SIR HANDEL

Brought up under instruction from Duke, Sir Handel can be rather bad tempered. Prone to temper tantrums, he is of the opinion he knows it all and should be the boss.

SKARLOEY

Always eager for work, Skarloey is a chirpy engine with a great sense of humour. With his good friend Rheneas, he works mainly in passsenger transportation.

STEPNEY

Saved from the scrapyard by Rusty, Stepney is always eager to please. He is enthusiastic about work and his engine friends.

A hard frost twinkled beside the track as Toby trundled purposefully to Mrs Kyndley's cottage. He had been sent with his faithful coach, Henrietta, to collect football shirts for a match that afternoon between Wellsworth School and a visiting team from the mainland. Mrs Kyndley had made the shirts herself and they were carefully piled inside Henrietta so that they could be delivered to the station in plenty of time.

"Good morning Gordon," said Toby as he pulled up to the platform.

"There's nothing good about it!" replied Gordon rudely. "I've been given inferior coal and now there's a blockage in my boiler. This shouldn't happen to an important engine like me!" he bellowed boastfully.

Gordon coughed and spluttered so much that a big, sooty cloud landed on the nice, clean football shirts as they were being unloaded by the guard. The shirts were now black instead of the team colours of white and yellow! Poor Toby and his driver didn't know what to do for the best.

Just then they heard a loud 'peep peep' as Thomas steamed into the station. "I think I can help," called Thomas, when he saw Toby looking so worried. Thomas'

Wrong Shirt

driver came over to speak to Toby and his driver. He explained that Thomas was taking a load of railway overalls to be cleaned before lunch and the football shirts could be washed at the same time. Toby was pleased and he waited patiently for Thomas to return with the clean clothes while Gordon skulked away, out of trouble.

Toby saw the football team from the mainland arrive for the match and he hoped Thomas wouldn't be too long. But he had no need to worry, Thomas soon came bustling back into the station in time for kick-off. All the laundry had been packaged neatly in brown parcels and the PE master had arrived at the station to collect the clean packages.

Toby and Thomas could see the football pitch from the station and they watched as the school team ran onto the field. Their shirts looked very smart indeed, but something was wrong. Instead of wearing a shirt, the goalkeeper wore a large, blue overall which was too long in the arms and legs and made him trip over. His

friends laughed but the goalkeeper showed them how the big overall would stop him getting mud on his hands and knees - he liked his new uniform. The PE master agreed they could play on, despite the confusion, and he blew his whistle. The engines went back to their work and the drivers chuckled to themselves about the mix up.

Later that afternoon, Thomas took the Fat Controller to the main station yard with Annie and Clarabel. He had almost forgotten about the incident earlier in the day.

But a strange sight awaited them at the yard. A workman on the line looked very uncomfortable in a young boy's football shirt. The Fat Controller wanted an explanation.

"There was no clean overall today Sir," said the workman, "just this shirt."

"Well, it's the wrong shirt!" said the Fat Controller crossly.

"Please Sir," interrupted Thomas. And he explained what had happened that morning and everyone laughed, even the Fat Controller!

Which two pictures of Oliver are identical?

Answers on pages 44 and 45.

Fill in the clues alongside the picture and the Fat Controller's real name will be revealed in the bold column.

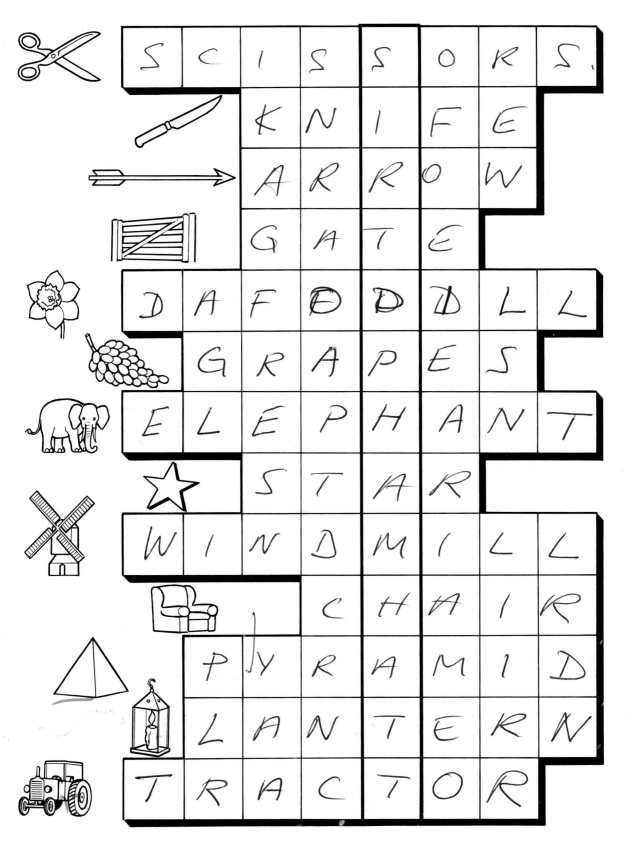

S	C	I	S	S	O	R	S
	K	N	I	F	E		
	A	R	R	O	W		
	G	A	T	E			
D	A	F	O	D	D	L	L
	G	R	A	P	E	S	
E	L	E	P	H	A	N	T
	S	T	A	R			
W	I	N	D	M	I	L	L
		C	H	A	I	R	
P	Y	R	A	M	I	D	
L	A	N	T	E	R	N	
T	R	A	C	T	O	R	

Thomas steamed out of his shed before the other engines were awake. Snow lay on the ground and he was very excited because it was the day before Christmas. Thomas liked Christmas. The passengers were always smiling and there were lots of special treats for everyone. Thomas didn't even complain when his uncomfortable snow plough was fitted.

It wasn't long before Percy and James bustled into the yard and there was soon a festive atmosphere as drivers hung holly inside the engine cabs and tinsel in the coaches.

The engines knew it would be a busy day and they soon set about their work.

"Goodbye James! Goodbye Percy!" Thomas peeped cheerfully to his friends as he left the yard with Annie and Clarabel.

By lunchtime, the snow had melted and Thomas waited patiently in a siding while his snow plough was removed. He watched the busy platform and was surprised to see a small black horse standing with all the people. 'That's unusual,' Thomas thought.

Imagine Thomas' surprise when he saw a passenger

speak to the horse. "How are you?" said the passenger.

"Very well!" replied the talking horse.

"Cinders and ashes!" exclaimed Thomas.

Back in the yard, Thomas told the other engines about the talking horse. But he wasn't the only one who had seen something mysterious that morning. "That's nothing," said Percy cheekily. "At Wellsworth station I saw a black pudding with blue flames coming off it. It was on fire, so I shouted 'Help!' but nobody paid any attention."

"Oh dear," said Edward.

"Well, imagine my surprise," interrupted James, "when I saw Gordon's guard with his daughter Nancy."

"What's surprising about that?" laughed Percy.

"He was wearing a flowery dress over his uniform!" gasped James.

The engines were used to seeing different things on the railway, but they agreed this was the most unusual day they had ever had. They decided to talk to the Fat Controller that night.

It was dark when the Fat Controller came to the yard. The engines whooshed and

chattered noisily.

"Quiet!" shouted the Fat Controller.

"You can tell me about it inside the big shed," he said knowingly.

The yard was filled with steam as the engines shunted noisily into the shed. When the steam cleared, they got a lovely surprise. The shed had been decorated and was filled with children singing carols. At one end, a stage had been made so a Christmas pantomime could be performed by the railway staff.

The engines watched happily, and quietly, until the end. Then the pantomime horse took a bow and Stephen and Bridget, the Fat Controller's grandchildren, stepped out of the costume.

"It's the talking horse!" cried Thomas.

At the end, a funny lady called Widow Twankey took a bow and her wig fell off her head. Then the lady took off her costume and underneath was a man they recognised.

"It's Gordon's guard, in disguise!" shouted James.

Finally, the shed door opened and the refreshments lady carried in a flaming pudding.

"Oh help!" shrieked Percy.

"It's a Christmas pudding," explained the Fat Controller.

While everyone ate their pudding, the engines agreed that pantomimes are a lot of fun.

43

Answers

Page 12

Page 13